WORSE THINGS HAPPEN AT SEA!

BOOK 1

Melvish Charts & Maps

GOING UNDER!

D1136068

Also by Alan Snow

WORSE THINGS HAPPEN AT SEA!

Book 2: The Worst Goo in the World

Book 3: Cheezilla!

HERE BE MONSTERS!

Book 1: Pants Ahoy!

Book 2: The Man in the Iron Socks

Book 3: Cheese Galore!

GOING UNDER!

WORSE THINGS HAPPEN AT SEA!

A TALE OF
PIRATES, POISON, AND MONSTERS

by Alan Snow

OXFORD

OXFORD
UNIVERSITY PRESS

Great Clarendon Street, Oxford OX2 6DP
Oxford University Press is a department of the University of Oxford.
It furthers the University's objective of excellence in research, scholarship,
and education by publishing worldwide in

Oxford New York

Auckland Cape Town Dar es Salaam Hong Kong Karachi
Kuala Lumpur Madrid Melbourne Mexico City Nairobi
New Delhi Shanghai Taipei Toronto

With offices in

Argentina Austria Brazil Chile Czech Republic France Greece
Guatemala Hungary Italy Japan Poland Portugal Singapore
South Korea Switzerland Thailand Turkey Ukraine Vietnam

Oxford is a registered trade mark of Oxford University Press
in the UK and in certain other countries

© Alan Snow 2011

The moral rights of the author have been asserted

Database right Oxford University Press (maker)

First published in 2010 as part of Worse Things Happen At Sea!
First published in this edition 2011

British Library Cataloguing in Publication Data

Data available

ISBN: 978-0-19-279272-3
1 3 5 7 9 10 8 6 4 2

Printed in Great Britain

Paper used in the production of this book is a natural,
recyclable product made from wood grown in sustainable forests.
The manufacturing process conforms to the environmental
regulations of the country of origin.

To Issy, whose father is not very good at drawing horses
& Theo, Maya, Finn, Tom and Ruby

CONTENTS

JOHNSON'S TAXONOMY OF TROLLS

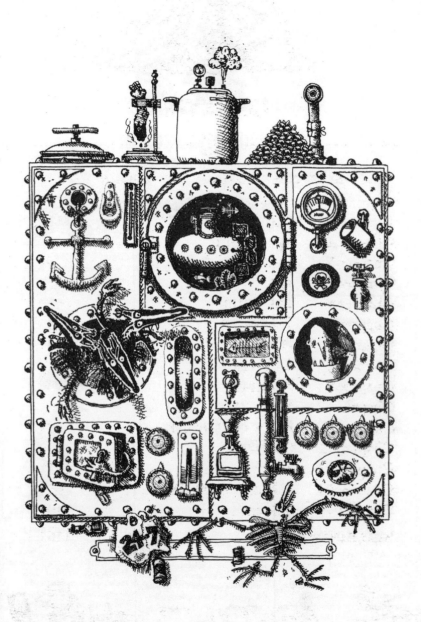

JOHNSON'S TAXONOMY
OF TROLLS AND CREATURES

Albatross
A true sea bird that has been known to spend up to 10 years without ever visiting land. Has large wingspan (3.5 metres). Can live up to 85 years and pairs for life.

Cabbage Island
A legendary island that is supposed to be in the southern Pacific. Said to be the home of strange plants with incredible powers. While it is not known if this island exists it is mentioned in many travelogues of the region and turns up in folklore surrounding cheese and health.

Crow
The crow is an intelligent bird, capable of living in many environments. Usually they are charming company, but should be kept from providing the entertainment. Failure to do so may result in tedium, for while intelligent, crows seem to lack taste in the choice of music, and conversational topics.

Boxtrolls
A sub-species of the common troll, they are very shy, so live inside a box. These they gather from the backs of large shops. They are somewhat troublesome creatures—as they have a passion for everything mechanical and no understanding of the concept of ownership (they steal anything which is not bolted down and, more often than not, anything which is). It is very dangerous to leave tools lying about where they might find them.

Cheese
Wild English Cheeses live in bogs. This is unlike their French cousins who live in caves. They are nervous beasties, that eat grass by night, in the meadows and woodlands. They are also of very low intelligence, and are panicked by almost anything that catches them unawares. Cheese make easy quarry for hunters, being rather easier to catch than a dead sheep.

Guillemot (paid entry)
Famously the name of the founder of the fabulous south sea trading company and mail order business. Providers of exotic and budget items for every home. Send a stamped addressed envelope and you will be amazed at just how quickly we respond (3 year delivery guaranteed).

The Members
Members of the secretive Ratbridge Cheese Guild, that was thought to have died out after the 'Great Cheese Crash'. It was an evil organization that rigged the cheese market, and doctored and adulterated lactose-based food stuffs.

Legendary Monsters
Often found wandering the southern sea and should be avoided at all cost, unless you are the owner of a Guillemot Monster-repelling Kit. These are available by mail order (see entry for Guillemot). These monsters are known to reside on many islands and thought to be the last remaining dinosaurs on the planet. Last confirmed sighting—Tokyo 1723.

Grandfather (William)
Arthur's guardian and carer. Grandfather lived underground for many years in a cave home where he pursued his interests in engineering. But after some rather unusual events both Arthur and his grandfather found themselves with a new home in the former petshop now rented by Willbury Nibble and shared with boxtrolls and Titus the cabbagehead. He now wakes up late, then spends his days in the company of Willbury and all their new friends, and has been known to sneak off on his own to the Nag's Head tavern for a crafty pint and bag of pork scratchings with a pickled egg. Now relieved of the sole care of Arthur, his favourite pastime is reading in bed with his own bucket of cocoa.

Shopping Birds
A once common bird that has now become rare due to its blatant consumerism and lack of intelligence.

Rats
Rats are known to be some of the most intelligent of all rodents, and to be considerably more intelligent than many humans. They are known to have a passion for travel, and be extremely adaptable. They often live in a symbiotic relationship with humans.

Trotting Badgers
Trotting badgers are some of the nastiest creatures to be found anywhere. With their foul temper, rapid speed, and razor-sharp teeth, it cannot be stressed just how unpleasant and dangerous these creatures are. It is only their disgusting stench that gives warning of their proximity, and when smelt it is often too late.

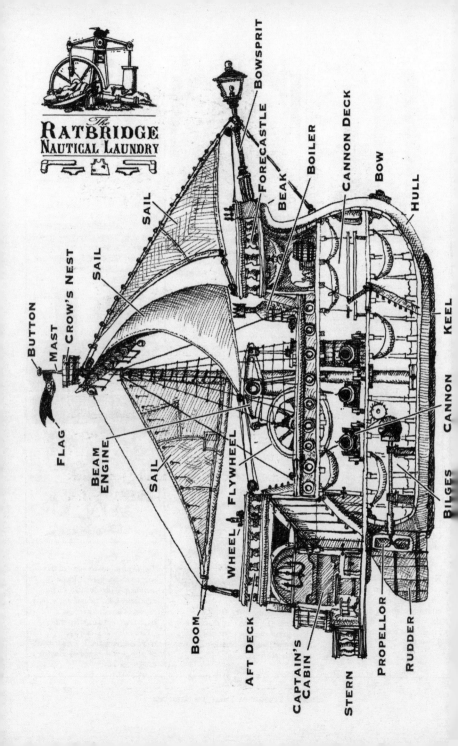

The Ratbridge Nautical Laundry

Chapter 1

DIRTY WASHING

Arthur and his grandfather were on deck, helping pack up piles of washing to be returned to the customers of the Ratbridge Nautical Laundry. Around them the rats and pirates were all hard at work checking lists, hanging out clothes to dry, and emptying baskets of dirty washing down the hatch into the bilges to be washed.

'Almost out of washing powder!' shouted a rat called Bert as he tipped a shovel of pink powder down the hatch after the washing.

He tipped a shovel of pink powder down the hatch after the washing

'You don't half get through a lot,' commented Arthur.

'Not surprising given the state of this place's underwear. Takes some shifting,' smiled Grandfather.

Then there was a commotion on the towpath. They turned to see policemen and an angry mob heading in their direction.

'What now?' muttered Tom, the worried-looking captain and laundry manager.

The police reached the gangplank and the unruly mob stopped behind them.

'String them up!'

'Hanging's too good for them!'

'Shame! Shame!'

Tom led the crew to the top of the gangplank to face the crowd.

One of the policemen came forward, pulled a piece of paper from his jacket, looked up at Tom and spoke.

Policemen and an angry mob

'Sir, are you in charge of this operation?'

'... Yes ...'

'Well, I hereby arrest you and your crew.'

'SHAME ON THEM!' cried the mob.

'What have we done?' Tom and the crew had kept the town's laundry and their noses clean ever since they had opened.

'Earlier this morning the famous Countess Grogforth visited the town on a ceremonial shopping trip and was shocked to see the town's underwear flying from your rigging in a rude display.'

'We're a laundry! It's just drying clothes,' Tom protested.

Kipper, the pirate by his side, was going red with indignation. 'Yes. And it's the town's clothes!'

'That is not my concern. Countess Grogforth passed comment on the unfashionable and coarse nature of the said underwear, and was so shocked that she fainted away, damaging her wig, her high born sensibilities, and the town's pride. She is now seeking compensation for that injury and the town is suing for damages to its reputation.'

The damaged wig

'This is ridiculous!' whispered Arthur.

His friends remained silent.

'As a law officer of this town I hereby serve you all with this arrest warrant and summons to appear at court at ten tomorrow morning. You're to remain here on the ship under police guard until we accompany you to court,' the policeman said. Then, pointing to the washing in the rigging with his truncheon, he added: 'And take that washing in or there'll be further charges.'

Leaning in towards the crew so that he couldn't be heard by the mob around him, he quietly added, 'Did you get the stains out of my vest?'

The stained vest

The police set up camp

Chapter 2

No Way Out?

The police set up camp at the bottom of the gangplank, and ordered the mob to disperse.

'On your way!'

The mob went quiet and looked a little uneasy. Then a rather runkled man came forward.

'Can we collect our washing first?'

Looking at how dirty the mob seemed, the officer nodded and a queue formed on the gangplank.

'Give them their washing.'

The crew did as they were told but this just added to their sense of injustice. As the last of the mob disappeared down the towpath Kipper shook his head.

'After all the trouble we take with their smalls . . .'

'Next time we should starch all their underwear.'

'There might not be a next time,' Tom said with resignation.

'Next time we should starch all their underwear.'

'What are you going to do?' asked Arthur. 'This is all totally unfair.'

'The first thing is to get hold of Willbury. He's a lawyer and will know what to do,' Grandfather replied.

'But we're not allowed off the ship,' said Tom, eyeing the policemen.

'We could attack the Squeakers, and throw them in the canal,' offered Bert.

'No, that would only cause more trouble. It would be better for someone to sneak off the ship, and go and tell Willbury what's happened.'

'We could attack the Squeakers and throw them in the canal.'

'But how?' asked Arthur.

Marjorie, their friend and chief laundry engineer, spoke. 'Wait until darkness and use the submarine?'

There was a raising of eyebrows. Although the submarine had been attached to the side of the ship ever since the crew could remember, it hadn't been used in years, and no one was really sure if it was still in working order. Marjorie, however, was not one to be put off by such concerns.

'I'll have a look at it and see if it needs any attention. It's moored on the other side of the ship, out of sight, and if we can get it going we can submerge, go along the canal to a place where the police can't see us, resurface, and then go and tell Willbury what's happened.'

'Sounds like a plan,' smiled Kipper, the largest of the pirates. 'Who is going to go?'

'Well I think I will have to,' said Marjorie, 'as I do know how to make the thing work, but I will need some help.'

Tom looked at Arthur and Grandfather. 'I think it would be best if we got you both off the ship. There is no need for you to end up in court.'

Arthur had mixed feelings about this. He agreed that it would be good to get his grandfather off the ship, and he had always wanted to have a go in the submarine, but leaving his friends to face the charges seemed a little disloyal.

Marjorie was watching him and spoke. 'This is a dangerous mission and I need you to help me drive the submarine.'

Arthur nodded and felt better.

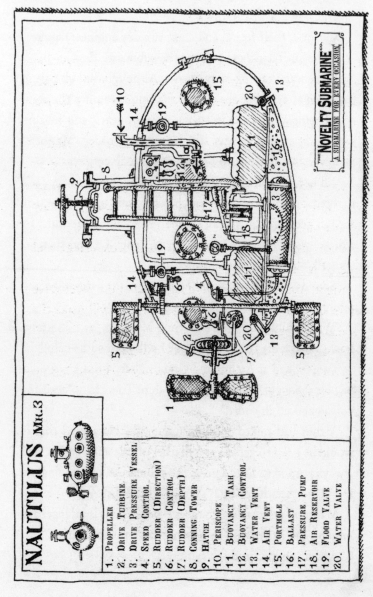

THE NOVELTY SUBMARINE CO.
A SUBMARINE FOR EVERY OCCASION

NAUTILUS Mk.3

1. PROPELLER
2. DRIVE TURBINE
3. DRIVE PRESSURE VESSEL
4. SPEED CONTROL
5. RUDDER (DIRECTION)
6. RUDDER CONTROL
7. RUDDER (DEPTH)
8. CONNING TOWER
9. HATCH
10. PERISCOPE
11. BUOYANCY TANK
12. BUOYANCY CONTROL
13. WATER VENT
14. AIR VENT
15. PORTHOLE
16. BALLAST
17. PRESSURE PUMP
18. AIR RESERVOIR
19. FLOOD VALVE
20. WATER VALVE

* * *

It took a few hours of secretive fiddling and preparation to prepare the sub. After finding the instruction manual, Marjorie was quietly lowered over the side with her toolkit and disappeared through the hatch on the top of the conning tower. By the time that darkness fell everything was ready.

Led by Bert, most of the crew then set up a distraction by pretending to play cards, while the group of submariners were lowered over the side and climbed into the tiny submarine.

Once inside the submarine Marjorie took charge and ordered Arthur to close the hatch.

'Right. Arthur, I want you to take hold of the water valve levers. They allow water into tanks and that will make the submarine submerge.'

'Not too deep I hope,' replied Grandfather.

'Not if Arthur is careful,' smiled Marjorie. She pushed up the periscope and looked about.

She pushed up the periscope and looked about

'OK. Motor started, and Arthur . . . open the valves.'

Arthur swung both of the levers and there was a gurgling from the pipes. They were on their way!

Arthur swung both of the levers

Up above the water, only the ducks noticed as a strange bent pipe started moving away from the back of the ship and heading off down the canal.

Only the ducks noticed

'I think we'll have to go quite a way under water or we'll be seen when we come up,' said Marjorie as she scanned the canal through the periscope.

The submarine moved slowly down the canal until they were well out of sight, but before Marjorie could give the order to surface there was a very loud CLANG! and the submarine stopped suddenly with an enormous jolt.

Inside the sub there were cries and yelps as the crew fell to the floor and the lights went out.

'What was that?' came Marjorie's voice.

'Is everybody all right?' asked Arthur.

'I think so. My whiskers are a bit bent but otherwise I'm all right,' Tom replied.

'Grandfather?'

There was no reply, and Arthur felt suddenly very worried.

'Grandfather? Are you all right?' There was still no reply.

'Marjorie, get the lights back on! There is something very wrong.'

They could hear Marjorie fiddling about and then a dim light filled the submarine.

Arthur turned to look at Grandfather where he lay on the floor. The old man had his eyes closed and was very still.

Arthur rushed to him and lifted his head from the floor. As he did so Grandfather started to stir.

'What's happened?' he muttered.

'We have to get him out of here. Can we surface?'

Marjorie was looking concerned.

'I hope so. We're far enough away not to be spotted by the policemen, but I don't know what's happened. Arthur, you close the valves and I'll fill the tanks with air to get us up.'

As the tanks were filled there was hissing, and a groaning from both Grandfather and the submarine.

Marjorie looked up the periscope. 'We're not rising. We

must be caught on something. Tom, have a look out of the porthole at the front.'

The rat peered out into the gloom of the canal water.

The rat peered out into the gloom

'It looks like a bedstead. It's caught around our bow.'

'Let's put as much air into the tanks as we can. That should do it.'

She moved a lever and there was more hissing and bubbling.

'What's happening with the bedstead?'

Tom looked out again. 'Seems to be holding us down.'

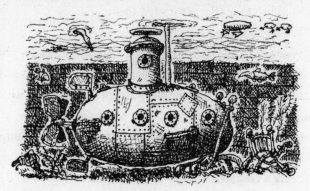

'It looks like a bedstead.'

Marjorie gave another push on the lever and the submarine finally broke free. It shot upwards, broke the surface and rose like a breaching whale, before finally splashing down and settling.

It shot upwards, broke the surface, and rose like a breaching whale

Again the crew found themselves shaken to the floor, but as Arthur was cradling Grandfather's head he managed to guard him from further injury—though the old man still let out a pitiful moan.

After taking a few moments to recover Marjorie climbed up the conning tower and opened the hatch.

'Let's get Grandfather back to the shop and find Willbury.'

It took a lot of effort and a great deal of care to get Grandfather out of the submarine and back to the shop, and by the time they had Grandfather tucked up in bed, Arthur, Kipper, Tom, and Marjorie were even more bruised and exhausted.

Willbury listened with horror to the happenings of the day as he tended to Grandfather.

'I will try to get time to prepare for the case once I have settled the patient.'

Tom and Kipper thanked him and then set off back to the ship with Marjorie, not really looking forward to the return journey in the submarine.

It took a lot of effort and a great deal of care to get Grandfather out of the submarine

Stuffed into the dock was the entire crew

Chapter 3

THE SCALES OF JUSTICE

As the last toll of the Town Hall bell faded at ten o'clock the next morning, the clerk of the court spoke. 'All rise!'

The court rose and all went quiet as in shuffled the decrepit form of Judge Podger. Stuffed into the dock was the entire crew of the Ratbridge Nautical Laundry and standing on the floor of the court were Willbury Nibble QC and Mr Smarmy Slingshot the prosecutor. Willbury was looking flushed, tired, and very glum after a bad night trying to tend Grandfather and preparing for the case.

He whispered to Marjorie, who was by his side.

'They're in for it. Podger will have them hanged if he gets a chance. I've had to try to deal with him before.'

As soon as the judge was seated the clerk of the court spoke again.

'The court may be seated. First case. Countess Grogforth and the Town versus The Ratbridge Nautical Laundry.'

'Very well,' Judge Podger said as he eyed the dock. 'Ten years each. Send them down!'

'Ten years each. Send them down!'

'SIR! I am acting on behalf of the Ratbridge Nautical Laundry and they plead not guilty,' Willbury protested.

'Damn you, man. I have a tea appointment at eleven.'

Mr Smarmy Slingshot now spoke.

'Sir, I would also like the case to be heard by your graciousness as both the Countess and the Town are seeking compensation for the criminal action of the members of the laundry.'

'Very well. But keep it short.'

'May I call the first witness, sir?'

'Get on with it!'

'Call the Countess Grogforth.'

The doors at the back of the courtroom opened and in walked two policemen supporting what looked like an Egyptian mummy. The policemen guided the mummy to the stand, where it curtsied to the judge and sat.

Mr Smarmy Slingshot began his questioning.

'Madam, can you tell me what has happened to you?'

The mummy made some muffled moaning noises and then went quiet.

The policemen guided the mummy to the stand

'As you can see, m'lord, the Countess is so injured that she is unable to answer any questions, but her very state is evidence of the great crime committed against her. I have no further questions.'

'Mr Nibble. Do you have any questions for the Countess?'

Willbury looked confused. 'Er . . . no, sir. Not if she cannot answer them.'

'Very well. Any more witnesses?'

'Yes, m'lord,' answered Smarmy Slingshot. 'Call Chadwick Spode.'

The police collected the Countess from the stand, and she was replaced by a small weeping man dressed in an emerald green and pink suit.

'Mr Spode. You are the fashion and society editor of the *Ratbridge Gazette*?'

The man nodded his head as he brushed tears away from his eyes with an orange hanky.

He brushed tears away from his eyes with an orange hanky

'Sir, speak up!' ordered the judge.

'I apologize on behalf of Mr Spode,' said Smarmy Slingshot, smirking at Willbury as he did so. 'He is in such distress that his doctor has given him orders not to speak, but he has prepared a statement for the court.'

Willbury stood. 'I object, m'lord. I have not been given a copy of this statement so have not been able to prepare questions based on it.'

'Mr Nibble! Objection denied. Given that he is medically excused from answering any questions I don't see it as necessary that you were given a copy. You are wasting my and the court's time and I will not take any further objections. Smarmy, please read the statement.'

Mr Smarmy Slingshot took a grubby piece of paper from the desk behind him and read.

Mr Smarmy Slingshot took a grubby piece of paper from the desk

'Dear court, yesterday afternoon I was working in my office when I heard of the huge disgrace that has been brought on the town. Ratbridge is a wonderful town and fine holiday destination, but it has been brought low by the criminal antics of the Nautical Laundry. How can visitors bring children here after hearing of the rude display of underwear, clearly visible from even several miles away. Our reputation is ruined. My social column in the paper will be a laughing stock. It may take years to recover from this outrage. Yours sincerely Chadwick Spode (GCSE English).'

Mr Spode was now weeping deeply into his hanky.

'M'lord, as you can see Mr Spode is sorely injured but this is nothing compared with the damage to the town's reputation. I ask that the court find the defendants guilty of all the charges and fine them an amount that will cover all damages.'

Judge Podger turned to Willbury. 'What have you got to say to that?'

'Sir, I would like to question the defendants.'

'I don't think so. How could we trust them? They will just give us some poppycock story.'

'I object, m'Lord!'

'I told you, Mr Nibble. No more objections or I will have you up for contempt of court. Any other witnesses?'

Willbury shook his head.

'Very well then. I order the jury to retire and bring back the verdict.' He then looked at his watch. 'You have three minutes!'

Willbury raised his hand. 'Sir, this really is outrageous! How can they make a fair judgement in just three minutes?'

Willbury raised his hand

'Silence, Mr Nibble. Given that the jury is made up from people of the town, I doubt very much that they will have any problem coming to the right verdict that quickly.'

Willbury was about to protest about the jury being likely to profit by a guilty verdict but as he opened his mouth to speak the judge cut him off.

'Just one word . . . ' and Podger ran a finger across his throat.

The jury didn't even take one minute.

'How do you find the defendants?' the judge asked.

'Severely guilty on all and more charges!'

'Good!' Then Podger turned towards the dock.

'What you have done has injured both the town and the Countess. And you will be punished to the full extent of the law.' He turned to the clerk. 'What is that?'

'I'm not very good at sums . . . '

Mr Smarmy Slingshot stood. 'If I may help. I have done some calculations based on lost trade, wig repairs, personal injury, and the price of dignity. I reckon it is about ten thousand groats.'

There was a sharp intake of breath in the courtroom and even Judge Podger raised an eyebrow. Then he smiled.

'Sounds good to me. I fine the Ratbridge Nautical Laundry ten thousand groats.'

Willbury raised a hand.

'Yes, Mr Nibble?'

'My clients do not have such money.'

'Well, they had better find it.'

'Where, sir?'

'That is none of my business. I shall give them six months to find the funds, and if after that time they don't deliver I shall impose long prison sentences . . . or worse!'

Ten thousand groats

Titus and the boxtrolls turned and smiled at him

Chapter 4

FINE!

At about the same time that the crew of the Nautical Laundry were walking out of the courtroom in a state of shock, Arthur was just emerging from his bedroom and creeping down the stairs. He'd been up very late. As he passed Grandfather's room he was tempted to check on the old man but there was a light snoring coming through the door so Arthur thought perhaps it would be better to leave his grandfather to sleep.

At the bottom of the stairs he crossed to the door to what had once been a pet shop, but now served as their living room and kitchen, as well as bedroom to Willbury and their friends Titus the cabbagehead, and Fish, Shoe, and Egg the boxtrolls. The door squeaked open and the familiar smell of bacon and cocoa hit his nose.

Titus and the boxtrolls turned and smiled at him, but he

could tell that they were worried.

'Have Willbury and Marjorie gone to the court?'

His friends nodded, and Fish, who was standing with a frying pan by the fire, pointed to some sausages and bacon in the pan.

'No thank you. I don't feel hungry.'

Fish pointed again and seemed insistent.

'Very well.' Arthur took a plate from Titus and held it out to Fish. Soon he was settled in an armchair eating while his friends sat about him and watched quietly.

Then steps and a key in the door broke the silence and Willbury entered. As he took the scarf from his neck he kicked the door closed, then turned to see Arthur and the creatures watching him.

'Sorry. It's just that damnable judge.' Then he looked upwards. 'Is your grandfather all right?'

'I think so,' said Arthur. 'I heard him snoring when I came downstairs. You're back very quickly. Have they delayed the case?'

'No. M'lord Podger has lived up to his reputation, and tried and sentenced in less than half an hour.'

'And?'

'He's fined them.'

'A fine. That's not too bad.'

'Ten thousand groats of not too bad!'

Arthur dropped his plate.

'Ten thousand groats!'

'Is your grandfather all right?'

Even the cabbagehead and boxtrolls understood this was a staggering amount of money and looked shocked.

'What are they going to do?'

'I have no idea but we'll get to that after we have sorted out Grandfather. Have you sent for the doctor?'

'No, I've only just got up.'

'Will you put on your shoes and go and fetch him?'

'I would . . . but are you sure he'd come? Grandfather threw him out last time after he turned up with leeches.'

'He turned up with leeches.'

'True . . . Maybe we should find another one, though they're all pretty useless.'

Titus, who had been listening intently, crept up to Willbury and pulled on his sleeve. Willbury looked down at him.

'What is it, Titus?'

The cabbagehead ran across the room to the barrel where he lived, popped inside, and reappeared with a copy of the *Ratbridge Gazette*. As he walked back across the room he opened the paper and searched for something. After scanning a few pages he found what he was looking for and held out the paper to Willbury.

Willbury took the paper and read aloud.

Willbury took the paper and read aloud

'"New Health Venture For All!
The people of Ratbridge will be
pleased to hear that a new doctor
(34) is to open a spa in our fair

metropolis. The great doctor goes
by the name of Doctor I. Snook
R. F. F. H. (28). Not only is this
great man (46) opening a spa but he
is going to offer free treatment to
all!"'"

Willbury raised an eyebrow. 'That's not going to be popular with quacks around here!'

Then he continued reading.

'"The Ratbridge Spa and
Alternative Therapy Centre is to
open on Saturday next and offer
the very latest in treatments
for the following illnesses—flu,
the common cold, athlete's foot,
tennis elbow, lice, measles,
housemaid's knee, and all that
ails the common man. And how is
this to be paid for, we ask? An
anonymous Ratbridge benefactor
(63?) is said to be behind the
scheme! When asked who this
philanthropic benefactor was, the
doctor (51) would only say that
the man was a retired local

businessman who felt that he wanted to pay back Ratbridge for all that he'd received from the town. Who could this be, we ask?

The Ratbridge Spa and Alternative Therapy Centre is to open in the refurbished buildings of the old Ratbridge public glue factory. And what treatments are we to expect? These the good doctor tells us are new, and fantastic, and based on a new remedy that he has formulated——a wonder drug that goes by the name of Black Jollop!

We here at the paper are not an easily impressed group of people and are ever watchful to protect the people of Ratbridge, so we sent one of our older hacks who happens to be blighted by gout, and often gets 'tired and emotional', to visit the new spa on a special pre-launch press day last week to try out the treatment for himself.

So did this Black Jollop fail to live up to the hype? Was our man left wanting?

Quite frankly we were amazed! He came hopping back to our office (quite literally!) and took everybody down to the local hostelry to celebrate and to give a demonstration of his new-found health. Not only was he able to walk there unassisted, but after several refreshments he danced on the tables in a way that many younger colleagues were unable to match. Yes! This treatment really does work.

So we recommend that if you are sick of pills for your ills and leeches in your breeches, you hop off to the new Ratbridge Spa and Alternative Health Centre at the first chance."'

He danced on the tables

Willbury stopped reading. 'This all sounds rather too good to be true. But they've nothing to gain if they are not charging for it . . . Maybe we should try it.'

Then he looked back at the cover of the newspaper for a moment.

'It opened this morning!'

Arthur looked at Titus. 'Well done.'

Titus looked very happy that he had helped.

'What shall we do then?'

'I think we'd better go and wake Grandfather.'

They all trooped upstairs behind Willbury and entered Grandfather's bedroom. Grandfather was no longer asleep and looked at them from his bed.

'How are you doing this morning?'

Grandfather was no longer asleep

'Not well.'

'We think you should get some medical attention.'

'Not that terrible doctor . . . ' Grandfather protested weakly.

'No. There is a new spa with what sounds like a fantastic new treatment that the paper says really works.'

'Sounds like some money-making scheme.'

'No. They are not charging for treatment.'

Grandfather thought for a moment. 'Well, it might be worth a try.'

'So then we need to get you down there. Do you feel up to walking?'

Grandfather started to lift himself, then fell back on the bed. 'Not really.'

Fish the boxtroll gurgled to the other boxtrolls. They smiled and all disappeared.

'I wonder what they are up to?' said Willbury.

After a few minutes Fish came back to the bedroom and beckoned Arthur and Willbury to follow him. At the bottom of the stairs was a wheelbarrow filled with cushions and blankets.

'They've made him an ambulance!' exclaimed Arthur.

It took a few minutes to prepare Grandfather for his trip but soon they had him comfortably settled in his 'ambulance'. The boxtrolls very carefully lifted the handles and pushed it from the hall, through the shop and out into the street. Titus walked ahead checking for any potholes and signalled for the boxtrolls to manoeuvre to the left or right. As they got ever closer to the old glue factory it became increasingly busy with people, all hoping for a cure for some ill.

Titus walked ahead

'Oh no! There's hundreds of them!'

Chapter 5

THE QUEUE

As Grandfather's barrow turned the corner of the lane that led to the old glue factory, it became clear just how many of the population of Ratbridge were seeking medical attention. The lane was crammed with the ill, injured, those who thought that they were, and some who were just worried about becoming so at a later date. Arthur looked in horror at the mass before them. There were those with bandages around various parts of their bodies, others were covered in spots and scabs, quite a few were supported by crutches, one man's nose had an angry-looking parrot attached to it and there were at least three children with their head stuck inside various pots and pans. It was not a pretty sight.

'Oh no! There's hundreds of them! We'll never get you treated, Grandfather!'

The journey had taken its toll on the old man and he was looking worse.

'What are we going to do?' Arthur moaned.

Around them the crowd was thickening and pushing them along.

'Stay together!' called Willbury.

Then some scuffling broke out quite near them. A large man with a brown paper bag tied around his head had tried to push past a group of old ladies, but they spotted him and set to work with their sticks and shopping bags in an attempt to drive him back. Another man thought he saw his chance in the distraction. He was in a self-propelled bath chair, and launched his transport at a small gap in the crowd. In doing so he managed to run over a bandaged gouty foot belonging to one of the town elders. There was a scream and more of the ill joined the scrap.

'Stay back!' warned Willbury. 'We must keep Grandfather safe!'

More and more of the crowd joined in the fighting.

More and more of the crowd joined in the fighting

Somewhat to Arthur's surprise it seemed to have a curative effect on a lot of the ill, with folks showing new-found vigour when facing queue jumping, or the chance to get ahead. A woman who was wrapped in bandages and had been lying on the ground moaning had jumped up and was now threatening to throttle anybody that tried to get past her with her dressings. Only by picking up the barrow and reversing out of the street did Arthur and his party avoid getting kicked or punched. The noise and commotion grew until it looked like a battle scene.

Then Arthur heard a loud whistle. He turned to look in the direction it came from and coming towards them were a large group of bicycle mounted policemen.

The Squeakers (as the policemen were locally known) threw down their bikes at the end of the street, and drew their truncheons.

'Riot positions!' ordered their officer. Immediately the Squeakers formed a line with truncheons raised high.

The officer blew his whistle as loudly as he could, and the sound reverberated off the walls of the lane, quieting the crowd.

'You lot have thirty seconds to form an orderly queue or you're in for a walloping!' he shouted.

The crowd didn't need a second warning. Immediately everyone stopped fighting and formed a neat line.

'I want a man every two yards along the street and if you see anybody try anything you have my full permission to . . . WALLOP!'

The Squeakers with truncheons held high

The Squeakers pushed down one side of the lane and took up their positions with truncheons still held high.

'What do we do now?' asked Arthur.

'Join the back of the queue?' offered Willbury.

'I suppose we'll have to, but it could take all day to get Grandfather seen.'

They took their place at the end of the line and began their wait. After a few minutes with no movement ahead of them Willbury spoke.

'I'll see if I can speed things up a bit.' He approached the Squeaker's officer who was still standing close by.

'Please. I have an old man with me who is really very ill and he needs to see a doctor right away!'

'Back in line!'

'But . . .'

'Back in line!'

'Please . . .'

Threateningly the officer raised his truncheon. Willbury backed off and returned to his friends.

'Looks like we'll have to wait our turn,' said Willbury.

Grandfather let out a pained moan. Arthur looked down at him and put a hand on Grandfather's forehead.

'He's very hot.'

'We've got to get you treated and soon. Most of this lot are wasting the doctor's time.'

Arthur was not sure that Willbury was being totally fair. There were a lot of people with fairly obvious illness and injuries, and after the fight there were even more, but he had to agree that it was urgent that his grandfather needed to see someone soon.

Looking at the queue he had an idea. 'I could try to sneak ahead, and get into the spa. Then I could ask if someone could see Grandfather straight away?'

Willbury looked around then whispered. 'I don't think that is going to be very easy. The Squeakers are on the lookout for that sort of thing.'

'I know. But we have to do something. I'm a lot smaller than most people here and if I got on my hands and knees I might be able to do it.'

Willbury looked at the crowd ahead of them. 'Do you really think you could do it without getting noticed?'

Arthur didn't feel sure he could, but he nodded.

'Very well. But I have an idea that might make it easier.' Willbury turned to Fish. 'Do you think you could make some very loud noise around the corner . . . as a distraction?'

Fish and the other boxtrolls gurgled to each other for a moment then Fish nodded.

'Well, you go off and get started; when we hear something Arthur can make his move.'

The boxtrolls scampered off and Arthur wondered what they were going to do.

While they waited for the boxtrolls to come up with something, Arthur tried to comfort Grandfather, then he noticed movement on the roof of the house opposite the end of the lane. A few seconds later he saw Fish's head pop up over the parapet and check the street below.

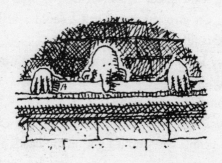

Fish's head popped up over the parapet

Then Fish disappeared and a moment later a large piece of guttering flew over the edge of the roof and dropped to the street.

CRASH!

legs of people at the very front of the queue and the wall. He looked about. A policeman was standing by the gates and was signalling to the people at the front of the queue to enter the spa as soon as any patient came out. Arthur watched. When he saw the next patient coming out of the spa he waited until they reached the gates and he pulled hard on the string.

A scream came from behind. 'THIEF! Someone is trying to steal my bag!'

As everybody turned to look, Arthur made his move. He jumped up and walked past the policeman.

With all the confidence he could muster he spoke. 'It's my turn now.'

The policeman just waved him through the gate

The policeman, distracted by the commotion, just waved him through the gate.

Arthur picked up speed and made for the front doors of the spa. He reached the steps, swung the heavy door open and was greeted by a voice.

'Welcome to the Ratbridge Spa and Alternative Health Centre.'

He swung the heavy door open

Two very slimy-looking men confronted Arthur

Chapter 6

TREATMENT

Two very slimy-looking men confronted Arthur. They were dressed in clothes that looked as if they had been stolen from a badly-dressed chef. And a very dirty chef too, for though the clothes might once have been white, they were now completely caked in filth.

'Can we 'elp you ... sir?' asked one of them in an oily voice.

'Yes. My grandfather's really ill and needs help. Quickly!'

'Where is 'e then?'

'In the queue.'

'Well 'e'll have to wait his turn.'

'You don't understand. He is really ill.'

'Did you hear that, Nurse Puggly? Tragic!'

Nurse Puggly was giving Arthur a funny look.

'Are you the young gent what lives with all them creatures and the old lawyer?'

*'Are you the young gent what lives with
all them creatures and the old lawyer?'*

'Yes. Why?' Arthur felt uneasy. How did the nurse know who he was?

'It's of no matter,' replied Nurse Puggly. He turned to his companion and spoke very firmly. 'Think we can make an exception here. Be tragic if one of this poor lad's friends was to get away . . . without treatment. We better take the young man to see the good doctor.'

A large hand took hold of Arthur's shoulder

A large hand took hold of Arthur's shoulder and he found himself being marched abruptly into the spa. Arthur felt confused for a moment, but the main thing was that he was on his way to see the doctor. Perhaps he would get Grandfather treated in time after all.

They reached the 'ward', and while his guards went to find the doctor, Arthur looked about what had once been the boiling room of the old glue factory. He was not sure but it looked as if very little had changed since the days of glue production. Large metal vats still occupied most of the floor space and pipe-work criss-crossed between them. The only concession to its new purpose was iron bedsteads filling every gap and absolutely everything had been badly painted a sickly pale green.

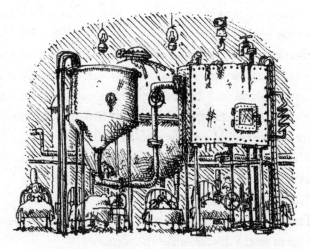

The only concession to its new purpose was iron bedsteads filling every gap

The only colour in the ward was the staff and the patients on the beds (and some of them were pretty green too). At the other end of the ward a crowd of the nurses were gathered about what Arthur guessed was the doctor—a very tall man pronouncing loudly about some patient who was hidden amongst the crowd. Even from where Arthur stood he could hear the diagnosis.

A very tall man pronouncing

'This is a case of terminal halitosis, and as you can see, the patient is in the latter stages of the disease. He would shortly go downhill and kick the bucket were I not to administer treatment. And does anybody have any idea of what sort of treatment we should give for such a condition?'

With one cry the nurses surrounding him shouted 'BLACK JOLLOP!'

'Correct. Hold him down!'

There were some muffled cries and then silence. After a minute or so the doctor broke the silence.

'There! What did I tell you? See! The colour is coming

back to his cheeks and the stench is disappearing!'

The crowd started to clap.

'Thank you, thank you. I know, I know! I just can't keep all this talent to myself. It just wouldn't be right. Now release the patient and send him on his way.'

The crowd opened to reveal the patient. Arthur could see the man smiling and watched as he tested his new breath on one of the nurses. This had no effect on the nurse and the man's smile broadened.

'I's cured!' shrieked the patient as he skipped past Arthur towards the exit.

'Who's next?' called the doctor.

He tested his new breath on one of the nurses

Arthur felt the hand on his shoulder tighten.

'Doctor! We have a lad here whose grandfather is in desperate need of attention.'

'Can't you see I have lots more patients waiting in the beds?'

'I think this might be more important. The governor

might be rather interested in making sure it happens.'

The doctor made his way over to Arthur and looked him up and down.

'What's special about him?'

'What's special about him?'

The nurse holding Arthur's shoulder leant over and whispered something in the doctor's ear. After a few moments the doctor raised an eyebrow.

'I think we must see what we can do then.' The doctor turned to Arthur. 'Well, lead us to your poor grandfather. We shall see what we can do.'

Again Arthur felt a strong sense of unease sweeping over him. He had never seen any of these people before, but they seemed to be singling him out for special treatment. Perhaps

it was just that they could see how very worried he was about his grandfather, and wanted to help him.

Arthur led the group out through the doors of the spa and back on to the street. The queue was waiting impatiently and when they saw the doctor there was a surge forward.

The doctor started to panic, then spotting one of the Squeakers he called out, 'Keep order! There's a very sick man out there that we need to get to.'

Several Squeakers came forward and raised their truncheons to make the queue part. Under the Squeakers' protection Arthur and the doctor's group made their way up the street to the place where Grandfather and the others were waiting. Willbury saw them approaching and was looking very worried.

'Not a moment too soon. He's had a turn for the worse.'

In the barrow Grandfather had his eyes closed and was shivering as Titus mopped the old man's brow with a cabbage leaf. Fish and the other boxtrolls were standing by the barrow and looking panicked.

'This is my grandfather,' said Arthur, pointing.

The doctor took a very quick look and spoke.

'Just as I suspected. In need of urgent treatment! Bring him straight to the main ward and I'll sort him out.'

Willbury came forward. 'I'm very thankful, sir. May we come with you?'

'Certainly. Wouldn't want the patient to be lonely, would

we?' the doctor replied. With this he turned back towards the spa and set off at high speed.

Brushing the others away the nurses picked the barrow clean off the ground and followed the doctor. Willbury took Arthur's hand.

'Well done. I didn't think you'd manage it. How did you convince them?'

'I'm not quite sure. They just seemed to want to come and help. Maybe they could just tell it was serious.'

'Wonderful! The doctor really must care.'

On reaching the spa the nurses had to lower the barrow to avoid banging Grandfather on the top of the doorway. As they reached the ward Arthur noticed that Willbury seemed rather surprised.

'Isn't it inconvenient having all this old equipment in here amongst the beds?' said Willbury, addressing the doctor.

'Quite the reverse,' replied the doctor. 'We need it for processing my wondrous cure.'

'In glue vats?'

'We did wash them!' The doctor seemed quite put out. Then he instructed the nurses to place Grandfather in a bed. There didn't seem to be an empty one so the nurses pushed an old lady with spots out of the nearest one and told her to find somewhere else.

'Are you sure that is necessary?' asked Willbury. The woman did look ill.

'Nothing is too much for such an urgent case,' replied the doctor.

There was a clearing in the centre of the ward between the biggest of the vats and in it were a large number of patients standing before a desk. Behind the desk were more nurses, this time with clipboards and spoons. Arthur watched as the attendants dispensed a dose of some foul-looking syrup from the barrel and gave it to another old lady at the front of the queue. She took the spoon in her mouth, made a horrid face and was about to spit it out when one of the attendants pinched her lips around the spoon and looked menacing.

'Swallow up!'

One of the attendants pinched her lips around the spoon

The old lady did as she was told. Then the attendant took his hands and the spoon away from her mouth and pointed her towards a bed.

'Lie down for ten minutes and you'll be feeling better.'

It was all the old lady could do to keep from bringing the medicine up, but she settled back on the bed with her hand over her mouth.

'Now . . . treatment!' said the doctor as he cast an eye over Grandfather. 'Fetch the jollop. Two spoonfuls I think. Nurses . . . hold him down!'

'Hold him down?' Willbury looked shocked.

'Powerful stuff, Black Jollop! The human body does not always know what's good for it.'

Grandfather tried to sit up but before he could move nurses descended upon him. Then the nurse with the spoon collected a dose from the barrel and came forward. As the spoon came closer a foul smell filled the air. Whatever it was, it had more than a little of the boiled cabbage about it, only worse.

'Oh God!' muttered Grandfather. 'Do I have to?'

'I think you must, sir!'

Grandfather opened his mouth and the first spoonful shot in. His face went white as he swallowed and he opened again. 'I think I would rather be . . . '

But before he could get the words out, a second spoon appeared and shot into his mouth. A nurse quickly pinched Grandfather's lips closed.

'How long will it take in a case like this?' asked Willbury.

The doctor smiled. 'Oh, you'd be surprised.'

'How are you feeling?' asked Arthur.

Grandfather reluctantly swallowed and the nurse released his grip.

'I'm not sure. There is a very strange feeling in my stomach . . . and it's spreading out from there . . . '

A smile broke out on Grandfather's face. 'IT WORKS! It really works!'

'IT WORKS! It really works!'

'What do you mean?' asked Arthur.

'I can feel the pain in my chest going.'

They all watched as Grandfather sat up and lifted himself from the bed. Arthur went to help, but Grandfather ushered him away. 'Let me do it. Do you know what? Not only have the pains in my chest gone but my hips feel better than they have for years. Remarkable!'

Grandfather lifted one leg from the floor and took a hop.

'Steady on, old man. Go easy!' said Willbury.

'It's fine. I feel fabulous.' With that Grandfather did a little dance. Everybody apart from the doctor was amazed. Grandfather tried a kick in the air and to his surprise his leg almost kicked Willbury's nose.

His leg almost kicked Willbury's nose

'I haven't been able to do that for years.'

'Take it easy!' ordered Willbury. 'You could injure yourself . . . or me.'

Arthur was overjoyed. He had never seen his grandfather like this, and joined in the dance.

'Dancing ain't allowed in the spa,' snapped one of the nurses.

The dancing stopped and Grandfather looked at the doctor.

'Sir, I want to thank you from the bottom of my heart.'

The doctor looked very pleased with himself. 'Not a problem. It would be churlish to keep all this talent to myself.'

'And coming out to fetch me before treating all the others.'

'When I heard you were connected with the lad I insisted that we give you top priority. It would be our benefactor's wish.'

Willbury looked puzzled. 'Your benefactor? Who's he?'

The doctor looked sheepish. 'A local businessman who wishes to remain anonymous. He's always felt that he wanted to pay back Ratbridge for what he's received from the town so he aids me with my research and with the funding for this fine spa.'

The doctor looked sheepish

'If he wanted us to have priority, as you say, he must know us, and presumably we know him.'

'Shall we just say that he has run across you in the past and believes you are deserving of special treatment. Beyond that I will say nothing.' The doctor put his finger to his lips and then smiled.

'Then will you pass along our thanks to him,' said Willbury.

'Of course, but do remember—it is I who have created this wonderful treatment.'

The doctor seemed a little put out that he was not getting enough praise.

'Of course, we cannot thank you enough, but do pass a little of the thanks on.'

'I shall. But now I really must get on, there are many others deserving of treatment.'

With that the doctor turned his back on the group and made off to the next case.

Arthur looked over at Grandfather who was smiling.

'He is a very odd man, and though he seems to have cured you I can't warm to him.'

'Great men are often a little strange. Never mind. Let's get off home and celebrate. I feel wonderful!'

The friends set off. This time Arthur rode in the wheelbarrow pushed by the boxtrolls. In the street outside they got some very envious looks from the queue, but Arthur didn't care. His grandfather was well again.

When they reached home Willbury disappeared and then returned with a packet of some rather special cocoa that he'd been saving for Christmas.

'This calls for a celebration. Fetch the bucket!'

'This calls for a celebration. Fetch the bucket!'

Jumping about like newborn lambs

Chapter 7

FIXED!

'I wonder if they'd give me a drop of that Black Jollop for my knees. They get a bit stiff when it's damp,' Willbury was musing over his cocoa. Fish and Shoe also seemed interested in treatment and gurgled while pointing to various parts of their anatomy.

'One drop of that stuff and you'll all be jumping about like newborn lambs. Get yourself down there first thing tomorrow,' said Grandfather.

Willbury shook his head. 'Better leave it to those in real need.'

The boxtrolls looked disappointed.

'I think we could go for a walk this afternoon to test my hips and to let the crew of the laundry know I'm all right.'

'And to check on how they are doing,' added Willbury.

The mention of the laundry brought everyone back down to earth.

'Is there anything you can do for them?' Grandfather asked.

'I might be able to appeal against the fine but I doubt I will be successful. Judge Podger is well in with the Law Lords and they are very unlikely to go against him.'

They set off to the Nautical Laundry in sombre mood. Grandfather did manage a few smiles along the way, but the thought of their friends' troubles spoilt the relief of Grandfather's recovery.

'He's all right!' came a cry from the bridge. Kipper had spotted them and had seen that Grandfather was recovered.

Soon the whole crew assembled to greet them and listened to the story of the Black Jollop.

'We were so worried,' said Kipper. 'That stuff sounds like a miracle.'

'That stuff sounds like a miracle.'

'It is indeed,' answered Grandfather. 'And I thank you for your concern, but you have troubles of your own.'

'Yes . . . ' replied Kipper and the crew suddenly looked very glum.

'Have you come up with any ideas as to how you could pay the fine?'

'Only one. We could sell the ship.'

'SELL YOUR SHIP!' Arthur looked appalled. 'But you are pirates. You can't sell your ship.'

'I think we will have to.'

'And even then we would be lucky to get as much as half of the money, so we would end up in prison in any case,' added Tom.

'We could do a runner?' suggested Bert.

'We have told you no already, Bert. We are not cut out for a life on the run and besides I think they would notice us trying to get the ship unstuck from the canal.'

'So . . . ' asked Arthur. 'What next?'

'What next?'

Quite a lot of arm wrestling

Chapter 8

AN OFFER

Grandfather and his new-found health took some getting used to and soon everybody apart from Grandfather was worn out. There had been walks, a visit to the swimming pool, dancing, and quite a lot of arm wrestling (which the boxtrolls enjoyed). Arthur noticed one other change in his grandfather—he'd lost his sweet tooth. In the past if cake or sweets were ever around Grandfather was never far behind. But now when cocoa and buns came out, Grandfather refused them.

'What's up with you?'

'I think it's my body telling me to eat well. I just don't fancy anything sweet since I got better. It's odd but I do have a desire for something, but I just can't put my finger on what it is. I'm sure it will come to me.'

Later that night Grandfather awoke in a sweat. As he sat

up in bed he found himself sniffing the air. There was a faint trace of whatever it was he couldn't remember earlier. He still couldn't put a name to it, but he found himself licking his lips as he settled down to sleep again. By his bed a pair of very muddy slippers sat in a small puddle.

Over breakfast the following morning Arthur noticed Grandfather looked preoccupied, but he snapped out of it when Arthur caught his eye and smiled.

'I am not sure why it is but I feel a little tired this morning. I have a feeling that . . . ' But before Grandfather could go on there was a rapping at the front door. Arthur answered it and was rather surprised to see the doctor standing on the doorstep.

'Can I help?' asked Arthur.

'I'd like to speak to my patient and that lawyer chappie.'

The doctor standing on the doorstep

AN OFFER

Arthur ushered the doctor into the shop and Willbury and the others stood to greet their guest.

'Welcome, doctor. Come to check up on your patient?' said Willbury with an outstretched hand.

This seemed to perplex the doctor but he nodded and shook Willbury's hand.

'Er . . . yes. How is he doing?'

'Very well, thank you.'

'Good. And I've come to ask for help.'

'Help?' asked Grandfather.

'Yes, help. Just like I gave you.'

'Of course. Whatever we can do.'

'The demand for Black Jollop is far higher than I ever imagined. Frankly, it is running out.'

'Oh dear.' Grandfather looked very concerned. 'You had better make some more.'

'That is the problem. It's not quite that easy. I need a certain ingredient and it's almost all gone. It is not a thing one can just get hold of. That is where you're to help. If I am to continue my good work you have to help me with some importing.'

Arthur thought this sounded a bit pushy.

'What can we do? We're not importers of anything,' replied Willbury.

'I am coming to that. I understand you're very good friends of the crew of that ship on the canal. I need them to make a trip.'

'So what do you want us to do?'

'They're your friends, aren't they? Get down there and tell them they are off on a voyage.'

'But . . . '

'Look here. I may well have saved this gentleman's life,' said the doctor, pointing rather rudely at Grandfather. 'Are you going to let me down when I need you?'

'No . . . no,' said Grandfather. 'It is just that it is not our ship, and they have troubles of their own.'

'This is a major emergency and if you let me down you'll not just be letting me down but also the people of Ratbridge.'

'I understand, but asking them to go on a voyage . . . '

'I'd think that it is the very least you could do for me considering that you might have died.'

There was a pause then Grandfather spoke.

'Very well. I'll ask them. But I'm not sure they can help us. Didn't you hear what happened to them in court?'

'Yes I did indeed. Sounded like they might be at a loose end now anyway.'

Willbury spoke up. 'And to where would this voyage be?'

'That is a secret. I have to closely guard the formula of Black Jollop. I'll provide someone to go on the voyage who'll know the destination.'

'The Ratbridge Nautical Laundry has to find money to pay off their fine, so why would they ever agree to going on a journey?'

'I have to closely guard the formula of Black Jollop.'

'To help you, the people of Ratbridge—and to earn ten thousand groats.'

'TEN THOUSAND GROATS!'

'My backer is so keen to spread the benefits of Black Jollop that he's willing to put up the money.'

'What do you think?' Grandfather asked Willbury. This seemed the answer to everybody's problems.

'TEN THOUSAND GROATS!'

'Seems more than generous.' Willbury turned to the doctor.

'How would we know that you would come through with the money?'

'Really! After all I have done for you. But what do you expect from a lawyer? Don't worry. I have a contract.'

The doctor pulled out a document from his inside pocket and passed it to Willbury.

The doctor pulled out a document from his inside pocket and passed it to Willbury

'It basically says that the ship and its crew will fetch supplies and in return shall receive the sum of ten thousand groats on return to Ratbridge.'

Willbury inspected the document.

'That is what it says. Also it hands captaincy and control of the ship over to you, though.'

'Technically that may be true, but my lawyers are insisting on it. If we are paying that much money we want control. The crew will be more than generously compensated for it. If they can do without the money . . . '

'I think we had better go and ask them. It's a lot of money.'

'Good. I shall expect to hear from you shortly. By ten-ish tomorrow morning if possible.'

With that, the doctor walked to the door. 'Supplies are running very short and there is already a queue outside the spa for when we open tomorrow. I must go and prepare myself to turn away the sick.'

The door closed.

It took even less time for them to agree

Chapter 9

FIREWORKS

It didn't take long to tell the crew about the contract and it took even less time for them to agree. Ten thousand groats was exactly enough to get the crew of the Ratbridge Nautical Laundry to sign the contract. There were still a few problems—how to free the ship from where she was stuck, the fact they were facing the wrong direction in the canal with no space to turn round, and how to provision the ship. Marjorie thought she had answers to the first two problems.

'I think there are three methods we could use to un-stick her. One: Pull her out. Two: Dismantle the bridge by hand. Three: Something a bit more interesting.' She smiled.

'What is the "something a bit more interesting"?'

'It's the most elegant and least tiring one.'

'What?'

'Wait for this evening. I could be ready by then . . . if I'm allowed to help myself to the stores.'

'Of course! Would you like any help?' offered Tom.

'No, I think I will be able to manage it on my own.'

'And what about the fact the ship is facing the wrong way up the canal?' asked Tom.

'Simple,' answered Kipper. 'Use the engine. It will drive us backwards, won't it, Marjorie?'

'Yes. All we have to do is put one more pulley in the drive train and she will go backwards all day. Might look a bit strange, going backwards down the canal. But once we get to somewhere we can turn round I can take the pulley back out and we can go forwards again.'

'Brilliant!' said Kipper.

Marjorie winked and disappeared below decks with a smile on her face. Tom then got out the chest where they kept their money and counted it up. It totalled eight groats and would barely cover a week's shopping, let alone provisions for an entire voyage.

Marjorie winked

'I'm not sure what we are going to do? Does anybody have any savings tucked away?'

After a few minutes the crew returned with another twelve groats in loose change, but it was still nothing like enough.

Willbury then came to their aid. 'I'll lend you the money on one condition. That I can come along!'

'Certainly!' smiled Tom. 'We would be more than happy to have you along.'

'Well I have one hundred and twenty-five groats invested at the post office—but it is my life savings and I really will need it back.'

The crew gave him a cheer.

'Do you know how soon the doctor wants us to set off?'

'As soon as possible.'

'When would it be possible to get your money?'

'All I have to do is get my pass book from home.'

'Would you like some of us to come along as guards?' asked Kipper. 'It is an awful lot of money.'

'Yes please.'

'Blunderbusses?' offered Bert.

A Blunderbuss

'I think that would draw attention to us and might also be highly illegal.'

'Shall I bring my cosh?'

'Very well. But you are not to bring it out unless someone else starts trouble.'

Bert agreed and Willbury set off with most of the crew in tow. As they walked they drew up a list of everything they would need for a long voyage.

As they walked they drew up a list

* * *

'Ready!' Marjorie shouted. It was early evening and after a busy day everybody was gathered on the towpath to watch. Marjorie ushered the spectators back behind a barrier she had erected some distance down the towpath, then she walked back to the bridge.

From where Arthur was standing he could see long sticks, each with a tube at the top, protruding from all over the bridge.

'I wonder what she is up to?'

'I am very sure we are going to find out, and very shortly,' smiled Grandfather.

Marjorie ushered the spectators back behind a barrier

Willbury was looking uneasy.

Then Marjorie came back towards the spectators, reeling out something as she did.

'What's going to happen?' Arthur asked.

'Watch!'

She pulled a box of matches from her pocket and leant down to the ground where the end of the string she had been reeling out lay. Then she struck a match and held it to the end of the string. After a few splutters the string caught light and there was a fizzling and a sparking as the fire rapidly moved along the string towards the bridge.

'A fuse! You're not blowing up the bridge are you?' shouted Willbury in horror.

'Wait and see!' she chuckled.

The sparkling reached the first of the sticks and things started to happen.

'Watch!' cried Marjorie in delight.

With a stream of flame one of the sticks shot high into the sky, then its jet fizzled out.

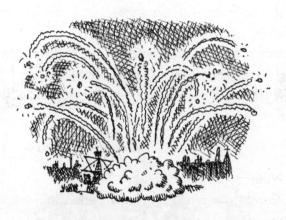

This was followed by another and another

This was followed by another and another. Some of the 'rockets' seemed at first to struggle to get off the ground, but slowly they all managed to disappear into the night sky. The display went on for minutes, slowly enveloping the bridge in a thick cloud of smoke. As it died away Willbury spoke.

'Very nice, Marjorie! Fireworks! But what about the bridge?'

'Wait until the smoke clears.'

Arthur watched. The huge plume of smoke started to drift off in the wind.

THE BRIDGE WAS GONE!

The applause died away and Marjorie bowed.

'Simple really. The rockets were fixed to all the stones that made up the bridge and POOF! Redistribution!'

Willbury looked rather unhappy, but not as unhappy as all the gardeners with greenhouses in Ratbridge were the following morning.

Arthur congratulated her. 'You're brilliant, Marjorie! There is nothing to stop us setting sail now.'

Willbury and Grandfather both looked at him, then at each other.

Not as unhappy as all the gardeners with greenhouses
in Ratbridge were the following morning

'I'm sorry, Arthur, but you are too young to go on this trip. You're going to have to stay here with me,' said Grandfather.

Arthur suddenly felt as though his world had collapsed. All day he'd been imagining setting off with his friends on the adventure and now in a moment it had been taken away from him.

'But Grandfather . . . '

'I'm sorry, I have discussed it with Willbury and he is of the opinion that this really isn't the sort of thing a lad of your age should be involved in.'

'Grandfather . . . '

'Arthur, that is an end to it.'

Arthur looked about at his friends the pirates and rats. They looked disappointed as well, but were keeping quiet.

'Maybe when you are older,' said Willbury.

This was the final straw. Arthur turned and walked away down the towpath.

Arthur turned and walked away down the towpath

Those cheeses that escaped made for the woods

Chapter 10
AN OUTRAGE!

The sky was clouded and the moon threw almost no light on the boggy marshes where the cheeses slept. The gentle but rather stupid creatures were slowly rebuilding their numbers after almost being wiped out in the days of cruel cheese hunting. Now of course that barbaric practice was banned. The sound of the water from the river mixed with the snoring of the cheeses, and masked the soggy footsteps of the approaching predators.

Then there was a crazed yell and the attack upon the innocent creatures started. From the darkness human shapes appeared and ran towards the panicking cheeses. The startled creatures took flight. But only the more mature cheeses knew the ground and were fast enough to evade the onslaught. As for the young and weak . . . there was little hope.

Those cheeses that escaped made for the woods, but were followed by the evil humans who'd been too slow to feast on the early victims. Soon these hunters were wandering about in the darkness amongst the trees, bumping into things and whimpering with their unfulfilled cheese lust. The trembling, terrified cheeses quivered in their hiding places behind trees and down burrows. After several desperate hours of searching the baying mob gave up and turned back towards the town, needing to get back to their beds before the night was over.

As the sun rose a lonely woman now reduced to doing her own washing settled a basket by the riverbank and looked about to find a suitable rock to scrub her clothes on. Her eyes fell upon something yellow, bobbing in the shallows. She reached down and picked it up. Turning it slowly in her hand, she began to shiver.

As she fell to the ground in a faint, her lips mouthed a word.

'RIND . . .'

Turning it slowly in her hand, she began to shiver

Titus looked a little shocked

Chapter 11

READY FOR THE OFF

Fish was standing by his usual place at the fire cooking breakfast when Arthur made his way down to the front room of the old shop. The boxtrolls and Titus were gurgling to each other excitedly, which made Arthur feel worse. When Fish held out the sausages Arthur shook his head and went to sit in Willbury's chair. For a few moments the boxtrolls went quiet but soon they started to gurgle on again. Titus offered Arthur a plate.

'Leave me alone!'

Titus looked a little shocked but backed off.

Then Fish came over and tried to console Arthur.

'Grumfff greee?'

Arthur pushed his hand away.

Fish pointed up the stairs and signalled Arthur to fetch Grandfather and Willbury for breakfast. Arthur lifted himself out of the chair and clumped up the stairs. He was about to enter Grandfather's room when he heard talking and stopped.

He heard talking and stopped

'I know Arthur really wants to go, but he really is too young.' It was Willbury.

'Yes, but they take eight-year-olds into the navy!'

'And look how they are treated! No! It'll never do. As his guardian you've a responsibility to look after him, and allowing him to go off on that wreck of a ship to some undefined destination is just not on. Imagine if something went wrong. How would you feel?'

'I know, I know . . . but you could keep an eye on him.'

Arthur was shocked. His grandfather would allow him to go. It was Willbury who was stopping it happening.

'Besides, who would look after you if you fell ill again?'

'I am sure I'll be fine—but if I took a turn for the worse I could find someone. We broke Arthur's heart last night when we told him he couldn't go. The experience might even be good for him.'

'Never! He's just too young.'

'Maybe if . . . '

'No! And let that be an end to it.'

Arthur heard Willbury making for the door and so rushed to make his way back down the stairs and sit down in the armchair again. This time when Fish passed him a plate of eggs and bacon, he reluctantly took it and started to eat.

He reluctantly took it and started to eat

'Ah Arthur! Just the person I wanted to see.' It was Willbury. 'Kipper and Tom dropped by earlier to tell me that the ship is ready. I want you to go down and tell the doctor.'

Arthur felt the food stick in his throat. He swallowed hard and didn't answer.

'Arthur. I want you to go down to the doctor to tell him the ship is ready!'

'All right,' muttered Arthur.

'Good,' said Willbury, then turning to the boxtrolls he added, 'Apparently they've made me up a real sailor's hammock.'

'You're going to have to muck in a bit with the crew,' replied Grandfather.

'I'm sure I can manage. I've never been to sea before. I'm looking forward to it.'

This was too much for Arthur and he put his plate down and headed for the front door. As he laced up his boots Willbury was telling Grandfather what the pirates had told him of their old voyages. Arthur felt sick. As he let himself out he heard Willbury telling of islands where giant tortoises lived, and others where there were huge birds that tasted delicious and you could just pick them up and put them in a cooking pot.

Arthur slammed the door.

Huge birds that tasted delicious

A large notice was fixed to the gates

Chapter 12

CAST OFF!

When Arthur reached the spa there was no queue. A large notice was fixed to the gates. 'Closed. We are unable to treat patients due to a lack of Black Jollop.'

He pushed open the gate and made his way across the deserted courtyard, through the main doors, and down the corridor to the main ward. The doctor was standing alone behind a desk stacked with strange equipment and seemed very preoccupied.

Arthur watched for a moment then coughed. This startled the doctor who looked up, quickly came around the desk, and placed himself between Arthur and the apparatus on the desk.

'What do you want? We're closed.'

'The ship's ready.'

'Good! Tell them I'll be along this afternoon. Now get out of here!'

Arthur turned away but noticed the doctor was following him. As soon as he passed through the gates the doctor closed and bolted them behind him. Arthur found himself alone again and feeling really miserable.

What now? he thought to himself. He couldn't face going back to the shop and in truth he was very curious to see how things were getting on at the ship. He decided to head for the canal.

The sight of the ship made his heart sink further. There had been a transformation. All its woodwork had been either washed or painted, sails had been taken out of storage and bound to the spars, new rigging had been put up, and the crew were now busy polishing, scrubbing or stowing things away. The ship no longer looked like a laundry. It looked like a vessel ready for the high seas.

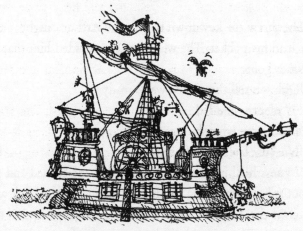

There had been a transformation

'Arthur! I've got something for you,' Marjorie shouted from the stern deck.

He looked up.

'What is it?'

Marjorie looked a little furtive and pulled out something on a chain.

'The key for the submarine. I've put a padlock on the hatch to stop anybody messing about with her while we're away. I want you to keep an eye on her.'

Something on a chain

She threw the key down to him and Arthur caught it and put it in his pocket. The weight of it reminded him that he was not going.

'Did you tell the doctor we're ready?'

He silently nodded.

'Did he say when he was going to get here?'

'No. Just later this afternoon.'

'I guess he'll just turn up.' With that she turned and set about oiling something. Arthur sat down on the bank and watched the clamour. After a while he looked across to the submarine. There could not be a greater difference between

the two craft. One looked full of life and the other old and dismal. Though he was now in charge of the submarine he really couldn't care less if it sank. He turned away from it and stared back at the ship.

What could he do? He had to get on the voyage. He stood and slowly crept up the gangplank, looking about. On one side of the mast was a large barrel. He walked over to it and lifted the lid. It was absolutely full of apples.

'Not thinking of becoming a stowaway, are we?'

He turned to see Willbury looking down at him. Arthur didn't reply.

'Don't think you can get away with any funny stuff. I shall be keeping an eye out for you, and making sure you're not aboard.'

Arthur dropped the lid of the barrel, and walked sulkily across the deck, down the gangplank, and off in the direction of the shop.

Off in the direction of the shop

At four the doctor arrived on a cart pulled by a very exhausted donkey. He insisted on being taken to the captain's cabin where he installed himself with his luggage. This consisted of about twenty very large trunks and cases. It took quite a lot of effort by some of the largest pirates to get them on deck, and down below. Though exhausted, the pirates offered to help him unpack but the doctor refused.

A cart pulled by a very exhausted donkey

'Don't worry. They contain delicate equipment I need for the jollop. I shall unpack them tonight.'

He then asked for the key to the cabin and locked it before joining the crew on deck.

Word had got around about the voyage and a crowd was starting to assemble to see the ship set off.

About six o'clock Grandfather heard a newspaper boy calling out in the street.

'Late edition! Late edition! Ship about to set sail! Black Jollop Voyage Special! Read all about it!'

'Late edition! Late edition!'

Grandfather went up and found Arthur in his bedroom.

'They'll be setting off shortly. Shall we go and wave goodbye?'

Arthur shook his head.

'Very well. You stay here then.'

'Why can't I go?'

'I've told you. You're not old enough to take care of yourself.'

'Who was it that helped save you in the submarine?'

'. . . you . . .'

'And last year who was it that saved the town from Snatcher and his men?'

'. . . you . . .'

'So I'm old enough to look after others but not old enough to take care of myself then?'

'I know it seems rough . . .' But before Grandfather could finish Arthur started again.

'So be truthful with me. How would you feel if you were my age and there was a real adventure about to happen and your grandfather stopped you from going?'

Grandfather thought for a few moments. 'Not very good, but I am only trying to protect you.'

'I remember you telling me loads of times that we learn from experience. And now you want to stop me from learning?'

'Of course not.'

'How old does the navy take boys?'

'Eight, I think.'

'Well, I'm ten. Perhaps I should run away and join the navy?'

'No! God knows what would happen to you if you did.'

'So it would be better if I learnt from people who cared for me, like Tom and Kipper?'

'I suppose so.'

'SO I CAN GO?'

'I didn't say that.'

'But can I?'

Grandfather looked the boy up and down. It was true that Arthur had already done much a man twice his age would have been proud of.

'You mean the world to me, Arthur. I couldn't bear it if I lost you.'

'You won't.'

'Please, please be careful.'

Arthur looked up him. 'What do you mean?'

'If you really want to go on this voyage . . . you go.'

'If you really want to go on this voyage . . . you go.'

'Do you really mean it? What about Willbury?'

'I'm your guardian, not Willbury. It might even be good for you. What is life without adventure?'

Arthur could not believe what had just been said. He grabbed a sack from the corner of the room and threw his clothes in.

'Better be quick! They could be going any minute.'

'Are you going to be all right without me?'

'Don't you worry about me. Let's get down there quick.'

Arthur rushed down the stairs three at a time, with Grandfather following. Even with Grandfather's new-found health and the fact that Arthur was having to carry quite a large sack, Grandfather was having trouble keeping up. Through the shop, out into the streets and towards the canal they ran. As they got closer the crowds started to hinder their progress, and they noticed something. The crowd were not going towards the mooring. They were coming away.

'Quick! They must have set sail,' Arthur called back to Grandfather. Then he reached the towpath and looked towards where the ship had lain. There stood the boxtrolls, but there was no trace of the ship—just the ruined remains of the bridge. Arthur followed the gaze of the boxtrolls along the canal.

In the far distance he could just make out a faint plume of smoke. They had gone!

Fish held up a finger and turned it in a circle

Chapter 13

SUNK!

'How long ago did they leave?'

Fish held up a finger and turned it in a circle.

'An hour ago?' Arthur panted.

Fish nodded.

Disappointment filled Arthur's heart and the tears started to well up in his eyes. The boxtrolls shook their heads, and Arthur started to feel sick. He put a hand in his pocket to reach for his hanky—and touched upon the key chain. He pulled out the key and looked at the submarine.

'I can catch them up . . . I'll use the submarine.'

'You can't. That thing will only get stuck again,' replied Grandfather.

'Not if I keep on the surface.'

'But you'll never be able to operate it on your own.'

'I'll need help then.' Arthur looked towards the boxtrolls.

Fish, Shoe, and Egg all took a step back.

'Please, please, I know you hate water but this is the chance of a lifetime for me.'

Arthur saw something in Fish's eyes glimmer for a moment.

'Fish, will you help me? You don't have to come to sea, just help me get it started. You boxtrolls are brilliant with machines.'

Fish was looking very nervous, but took a gulp, then a step forward, and nodded.

Arthur grinned from ear to ear, while the other boxtrolls looked horrified.

'Come on then!' Arthur jumped on to the roof and unlocked the hatch. Reluctantly Fish stepped over the gap, and hung on to Arthur. As soon as the hatch was open Arthur pushed the Boxtroll up and into the tower.

Fish stepped over the gap, and hung on to Arthur

'You go steady my boy, and take care!' called Grandfather from the bank as Arthur climbed in after Fish.

'I will. And you look after yourself,' Arthur beamed back. 'Cast off . . . please.'

With the aid of the remaining Boxtrolls, Grandfather freed the submarine and waved them off.

Inside, Fish seemed a little happier. It was bone dry, warm, and the smell of oil settled him. After looking about and taking in the machinery he prepared himself.

'Ready?' asked Arthur as he watched Fish from above. The Boxtroll gave Arthur a wink and the motor started.

'Here we go!'

The little submarine started down the canal

The little submarine started down the canal. Arthur stood with his head out of the conning tower, calling down instructions for steering, and soon they were almost out of sight of Grandfather and the other boxtrolls. Arthur returned their waves until he could see them no more.

'I heard Kipper say that they were going to stop in Bristol tonight so we can catch them up there. Do you think you could work out how to submerge this thing, Fish?'

Fish came to the bottom of the ladder and looked up at Arthur.

'It's just I don't want Willbury to see us. If I can climb on board and hide until they are out to sea, they are not going to turn round just to drop me off, are they?'

Fish smiled and nodded.

Fish smiled and nodded

The ship had tied up on Bristol's main quay for the night

Chapter 14

A Farewell to Harbour

The ship had tied up on Bristol's main quay for the night and the crew had gone ashore for a last drink before the voyage. Willbury had joined them for a sherry and had even asked the doctor to come along for one, but he had refused, saying that he needed to prepare the maps for the voyage.

At daybreak the crew assembled on deck. Tom was still acting as captain and stood at his post on the bridge with a pilot who had come aboard to guide them out of harbour.

'Order of the day?' asked Kipper.

'We are going to use the steam engine until we get out into the channel. Then after we have dropped the pilot off, we'll put up the sails and off we go!'

Tom at his post with the pilot

There was a cry from the deck. 'When's breakfast?'

It was the doctor. He was dressed in a huge pink dressing gown and slippers.

'Kipper, will you see to our guest!' ordered Tom.

Kipper took him down to the galley and told him to help himself to porridge and treacle. A few minutes later Kipper returned to find the saucepan gone, along with the large jug of treacle. Later still Kipper found the empty pan and jug on the sideboard in the kitchen.

'Big eater, that doctor. Wouldn't have thought it to look at him.'

Soon they were out in the channel

Tom gave the order to cast off. The beam of the engine started to rise and fall and the ship moved slowly out from the harbour wall. Soon they were out in the channel and making their way down towards the sea. The morning tide was with them and they made good progress. After an hour under the guidance of the pilot, they reached the estuary and the pilot was taken off in a small boat.

The pilot was taken off in a small boat

As they were now free of the channel and in a fresh breeze, Tom ordered the sails be hoisted. There were happy cries at this as the crew had not been under sail for a long time now and a good wind in sails is something that brings real joy to a sailor.

'Feels great, doesn't it!' Tom called to Kipper.

'Blooming fantastic!'

Shortly the doctor appeared fully dressed.

'When do you think we will reach international waters?' he asked.

Tom was surprised by the question but asked Marjorie, who was acting as navigator.

'I think about three hours.'

'Do you think you could let me know when we are there?' asked the doctor.

'Yes. But why?'

There was no reply. The doctor had disappeared below.

'I wonder what's on his mind?' said Tom.

'Probably worried about it getting rough as the waters get deeper.'

The wind picked up and the ship started to surge forward.

After an hour or so the doctor reappeared and asked if there was a snack he could have.

'After all that porridge?' sputtered Kipper.

'I think it must be the sea air.'

Kipper took him down below again and gave him a large cake tin full of bread pudding.

'That should keep you happy.'

The doctor opened the tin and smiled. 'Well, it should do for the moment. What time is lunch?'

'What time is lunch?'

'Have you got hollow legs?'

'Something like that.'

At twelve Marjorie took a reading with the sextant and started to work out their position. They could just about still see land, but she wanted to get into practice. While she was doing the calculations lunch was served, and the doctor disappeared with another tray full of food.

At twelve Marjorie took a reading with the sextant

Marjorie enjoyed the maths for the calculations and took another reading an hour or so later when land had disappeared. After some time with a book of tables and a chart she declared that they were now in international waters.

'Shall I go down and tell the doctor?' asked Kipper. 'Perhaps he'd like to celebrate with a little snack.'

'I think it would be courteous,' replied Tom.

Kipper headed below, and then returned. 'He says he will be up in a few minutes . . . with a little surprise for us.'

'Oh goodie. I love surprises,' chirped Tom.

'I've lined up a little surprise for you all.'

Chapter 15

SURPRISE!

The doctor appeared, made his way to the bridge, and spoke to Tom.

'I've lined up a little surprise for you all.'

'That is very kind of you. There was no need.'

'It would make me very happy if you would indulge me in my little eccentricities.'

'I am sure we can do that,' said Marjorie.

'I would like the surprise to have its full effect. Would you mind ordering everybody on deck and joining them there? Then I want everybody to close their eyes and turn away while I get everything ready.'

This seemed like great fun. Tom asked the doctor to hold the wheel, then he marched to the edge of the bridge.

'All hands on deck . . . for a surprise!' The crew assembled, and Tom, Kipper, and Marjorie joined them.

'The doctor wants to give us all a big surprise. We've to turn our backs and close our eyes.'

They did as they were told.

'Keep your eyes closed and count to a hundred,' the doctor called out.

The crew started to count aloud.

'No peeping!'

'No peeping!' added the doctor.

As the counting reached ninety, everybody was just bursting with excitement.

'Ninety-one, ninety-two, ninety-three, ninety-four, ninety-five . . . ' Some of the crew almost passed out with excitement. ' . . . ninety-six, ninety-seven, ninety-eight, ninety-nine, one hundred!'

The crew all spun round to find themselves facing fifteen blunderbusses, five trotting badgers, twenty men in tall hats and grubby suits and, standing at the front of this mob, one particularly unpleasant-looking failed ex-cheese merchant and master criminal with a grin right across his face.

'Surprise!' smirked Archibald Snatcher.

'Surprise!'

NOCENS SENTENTIA PRO IGNARUS

1 GROAT

THE ·Ratbridge·Gazette·

CHEESE ATTACKED!
WOMAN CHARGED.

A Mrs Fingle (52) of Innox Rd, Ratbridge, was found asleep this morning on the banks of the River Rat amongst the savaged remains of a CHEESE! Pieces of RIND bearing the evidence of human tooth marks lay strewn about the ground where she lay. Once awoken the

guilty woman denied the crime. Police have locked Mrs Fingle (38) up, and she is to appear before magistrates later today.

We thought the barbaric & medieval practice of consumption of cheese would have been stopped by the outlawing of cheese hunting, but yet again the law is flouted. This paper will campaign for the heaviest of sentences for those who take it upon themselves to prey on these defenceless creatures. Cheese hunting and eating has to be stamped out!*

*detailed engravings of the terrible crime scene and gory reconstructions of her savage acts of bestial cheese eating on pages 2,4,5,7,9.10,11, and 14, and you can read more in a special Cheese Crime edition tomorrow morning.

DOCTOR SAVES TOWN WITH WONDER CURE!

Hundreds of Ratbridge's townsfolk have been cured of their ills by recently arrived Dr I. Snook, and his wonder drug 'BLACK JOLLOP'. The cure-all dispensed by this modern day saint from his newly opened Spa and clinic, is, he says, only

paying back a debt he says the people of the town are owed.

What has Ratbridge done to deserve such a wondrous thing? The doctor would not say as he dispensed free treatment to all those in need. And there were many

of them! In fact so many that the supply of
Black Jollop is now exhausted! What is to
be done? How are those afflicted by ills
to be cured? Must the Doctor's work come
to an untimely end?

No, for coming to his aid are the crew
of the Ratbridge Nautical Laundry who
offered to set sail to fetch supplies of
the key ingredient from a source in the
southern seas. Amid scenes of jubilation
the Laundry cast off from its position in
the canal last evening and set sail on its
voyage. May the winds speed their passage
and fortune guide their path!

**Mangled Marrows or Crushed Chrysanthemums?
See inside for full story of mass destruction of
town's greenhouses.**

WHAT HAPPENS NEXT ...

The story continues in book 2, *The Worst Goo in the World*. Evil ex-cheese merchant, Archibald Snatcher, is back, and he's taken over the *Nautical Laundry*! Now Marjorie the inventor, Willbury Nibble, and the ship's crew are at the mercy of Snatcher and his men. But what do they want? And can secret stowaways Arthur and Fish organize a mutiny?

Read the next gripping instalment of *Worse Things Happen at Sea!* to discover the answers to all these questions and more ...

How long can Arthur and Fish stay undetected in the barrel—and what can they do to outwit the awful Snatcher and his men?

Why has Snatcher returned—and what is he up to?

Will the crew manage to survive on measly rations of worm-infested hardtack?

J ust why does Snatcher dress up as an ancient sea god?

W hat is really in Black Jollop,

and the worst goo in the world?

C an a bacon sandwich be an instrument of torture?

A nd how did the doctor get mixed up in all this?

The History of the Ratbridge Nautical Laundry

For a number of years before the Laundry arrived in Ratbridge, it had operated as a pirate ship around the English and European coasts. It was not a terribly profitable enterprise, but it did survive. The crew were not a brave bunch and fighting was not really their thing. They liked the idea of being pirates and rather enjoyed dressing up and sailing, but going up against those who would not willingly part with their possessions seemed very disagreeable. It meant a lot of trouble and people getting hurt. No, they preferred trading in second-hand goods. These they would get from jumble sales in village halls in the various ports that they visited. As sailors most of them had learnt to sew and mend and this meant they were well equipped to recondition things.

For a long time this raised an adequate income to live on, but jumble sales slowly became less frequent, and a new trend started for cart sales. These were sales where people would load up their carts with anything they wanted to get rid of, and assemble in a field. Other people would then come to the field and buy whatever they fancied. This was harder for the pirates as the sales were usually held out of town and the pirates didn't have transport to get about on land. Tension grew over the months and tempers frayed as the budget got tighter. This finally came to a head with the food...

The ship's cook was a little brighter than most of those on board and spent most of his energy trying to make extra money by embezzling the food fund. He did this by substituting ingredients in his preparation of the rations. His name was Pungent. Pungent had a great imagination and he used this to create dishes that might (if good ingredients had been used) have been quite nice.

But by cutting every corner in the making of them he produced only the vilest of dishes. In fish pie he would substitute seaweed for fish. This he would cook until it no longer had any colour and was so mushy that it could not be distinguished from fish that had also been boiled for as long. Instead of making a white sauce with butter, flour and milk, he would boil sawdust until it produced thin milky glue. Then instead of a cheese and potato topping he would boil socks down to make a flavouring that he added to recycled newspaper. The finished pie looked quite like a fish pie. It even had a vaguely cheesy smell, but it was certainly not fish pie and it tasted disgusting.

One of the things that sailors tended to live on was ship's biscuits. Most sailors had grown up with them and it was to these that the pirates turned when they found everything else inedible. Ship's biscuits were cheap to produce but Pungent could not bear to let another opportunity for profit go by. The ingredients should be flour and salt. These were made into stiff dough, rolled out flat, baked, and then left to dry out until very, very hard. But even with so cheap a recipe Pungent went to town. Over the months he reduced the amount of flour he used, replacing it with anything he could.

Finally he went too far.

Things had been bad on the jumble sale front for several weeks, and the crew were restless. Pungent was wandering the docks when he came across the remains of a piano. He had found that sawdust often worked very well as a replacement for flour in the biscuits—and here was something largely made of wood. Getting it on to the ship was no problem, breaking it up in grindable bits was no problem, but it was covered in black lacquer. He decided that he would tell the pirates that he had used whole grain flour.

That ought to satisfy them if they asked questions. He put the wood through the mincer, then decided to bulk it up by throwing in all the ivory keys. The mincer produced a large pile of 'flour'. It had the faint odour of burning hair. Pungent added some seawater to the mix. After ten minutes of stirring he had produced a large grey ball. He squashed it out on the floor with his bare feet, and then cut it up into slabs. After putting them in the stove he turned up the heat and went to sleep in his hammock.

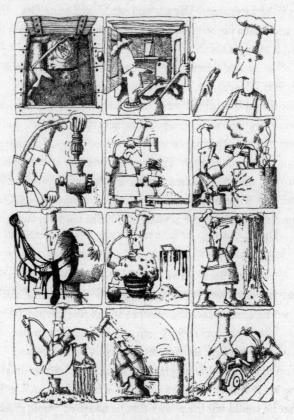

As lunchtime approached he took the biscuits out of the stove, retching at the appalling smell. He looked at them with pride—all grey and oily, with what looked like little teeth glinting in them. For the pirates' lunch, he knocked together a mixed grill from pieces of rubber boot and fried string. He placed the 'food' on a large salver and put it on the dining table in the main cabin. As usual the pirates reluctantly wandered in and sat down. Each took a few pieces of the fry-up and tried to eat. Each in turn gave up. Then came the usual cry.

'Where are the ship's biscuits? I am not eating this!'

Pungent went to the galley and brought out the new biscuits. Hands shot out and grabbed the biscuits. Then all was silent for a moment.

'Oi! My biscuit has bitten me!'

'So has mine!'

'Me too!'

'What has he done with our biscuits?'

'It's ornamentation! I just thought you would like something a bit different.'

'I'll give you something a bit different!'

The pirates lost no time in avenging their truly awful supper. What followed was not pretty. Pungent received a large number of bruises from the flying biscuits and was then dragged on deck. It took a lot of persuasion by the captain to stop the crew from keelhauling Pungent. It was finally decided to maroon him.

'Where we going to do that then?'

'The Isle of Wight is only about two hours away.'

And so it was decided to leave him there. When he had been put in an open boat with his own mixed grill he was set off and a party started. Over the course of the next few hours the pirates got very drunk and rather loud. Unlike many ships of its day, the *May Lou* had an engine and into its boiler the biscuits were thrown.

The party went on and as the biscuits burned the ship made good speed, unnoticed by the crew, on a path of its own choosing. The crew finally fell asleep and still the ship steamed on. Then it stopped.

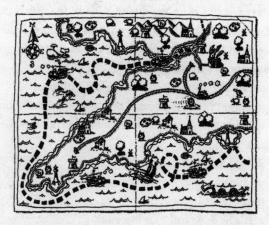

The next morning a mast flying a skull and crossbones was seen rising from behind the Ratbridge Gristle works. Word spread about the town like wildfire and soon more than half the town set off to find out more. A crowd had assembled on the canal bridge and along the towpath. For there—stuck under the bridge—was the front of a large ship.

Before long the hubbub of the crowd woke the crew from their slumbers. Groggy from their deep sleep, it took them some time to understand what had happened to their ship.

Optimistic at first, the crew set to and tried to free the ship, but to no avail. The crew then assembled on deck and a meeting was held.

'Well, it seems that we are stuck and broke!' said the captain.

'What are we going to do then?'

'Well, it's a Tuesday, and there won't be any jumbles till Saturday, and we have to eat. I suggest that we put our thinking hats on and try to think of some way to get ourselves out of this mess.'

'Well, let's look at what we know we can do?'

'We can plunder!'

'No, we can't! We are rubbish at that!'

'We could offer boat trips!'

'We're stuck, stupid! Boat trips mean moving!'

'We could open a laundry!'

All fell silent again

'Yes,' said the captain. 'We could open a laundry!'

Follow the rest of the story in:

Book 2

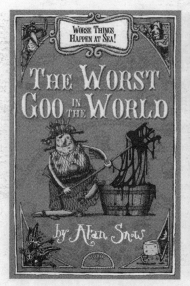

Book 3

ISBN 978-0-19-279273-0   ISBN 978-0-19-279274-7

Available now!

Join Arthur and his friends in the first
wonderfully weird Ratbridge Chronicles
adventure, HERE BE MONSTERS!

Book 1   **Book 2**   **Book 3**

   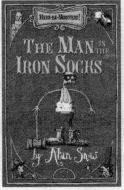   

ISBN 978-0-19-275540-7   ISBN 978-0-19-275541-4   ISBN 978-0-19-275542-1

Beneath the streets of Ratbridge, something is
stirring ... It is up to Arthur, prevented from going
home by the evil Snatcher, to save the day.
With the help of Willbury Nibble QC (retired),
a band of boxtrolls, some cabbageheads, and Marjorie
the inventor, can Arthur keep Ratbridge from
danger—and find his way home?